Cassidy

and the

Lost Fairy

of Allerton

Written by Jillian Duchnowski
Illustrated by Ana Stojkanović

Dedication

To my husband, Rob, whose imagination I love seeing at work (even with those awful puns) and who unfailingly encourages and supports my creative pursuits—J.D.

I love hearing from readers and seeing photos of families reading my book. Please connect at:
facebook.com/jillianduchwrites
Instagram: @jillianduch
Twitter: @jillianduch
Newsletter: //bit.ly/368gbCP

May you always see the magic around you.
-Jillian

Cassidy was bored. She didn't want to play with her dolls. She didn't want to play soccer with Daddy. She definitely didn't want to go for a walk, but Mommy ushered her to the car.

Soon, they arrived at Allerton Park. It wasn't like any park Cassidy had ever seen. Mommy and Daddy said it would be fun to see statues and pretty flowers, but Cassidy just pouted. She sighed loudly. She dragged her feet.

Tears threatened to spill down her cheeks, and, before long, Mommy and Daddy were walking far ahead of her.

Cassidy looked up at the sky and saw blue. She studied the feather-delicate tips of the evergreen trees. She watched how her pink shoes hit the gravel walkway. Then, she looked to her right and saw...

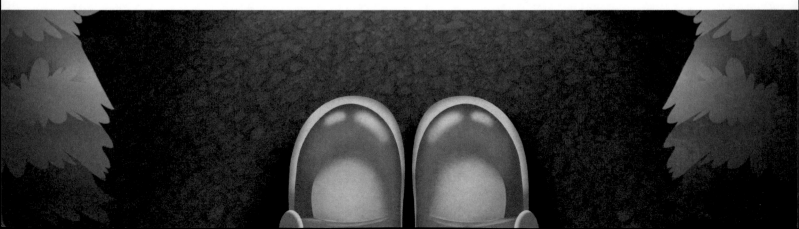

A fairy peeking out from the hedge and looking at her! She watched as the fairy's wings fluttered like a hummingbird's. The fairy beckoned Cassidy to follow and disappeared deeper into the hedge. Cassidy glanced over her shoulder and dove in after her.

She spotted the fairy perched on a bare branch. The hedge branches criss-crossed so it was hard for Cassidy to move, but she crawled as close as she could. The fairy, swinging her legs, spoke very, very softly.

"My name's Dayana. DAY-ana. Not too many humans come in here but I figure it's okay for one human child to see me."

"I almost can't believe I'm seeing you," Cassidy admitted. "Where did you come from?"

"All the way from Germany. Back when I was 223 years old..."

Cassidy gasped. "How can you be that old?"

"I'm 344 years old now. I am still a very young fairy. See? My wings still have bright colors. That's how you can tell."

"Wow. I'm just eight," Cassidy replied.

"Anyway, in Germany, my friends and I were exploring a market when a terrible storm blew in. My friends slipped into a carriage to stay dry, but the driver closed the door just before I could enter."

"I flew this way and that, my wings beating so quickly no human could see them. Finally, I winked my right eye twice so I could shrink even smaller and then I darted right into a man's pocket."

"That's a silly place to hide," Cassidy said, giggling.

"Fairies sometimes do silly things," Dayana nodded. "But I decided to stay with him for a while. The beauty I saw in flowers, he found in things humans made. He was absolutely obsessed with looking at art.

From his pocket, I saw dozens of paintings and sculptures."

"One day, I fell asleep in his boot. He had left them by the fire, and they were so warm and cozy. When I awoke, I was in the United States. In Illinois. At a house not far from here."

"Weren't you afraid?"

Dayana's head fell before she answered: "I flew all around but I could not find any fairies here. All I saw was a rectangular pond for the humans and a little lake where dozens of fish swam.

"I flew and flew and flew until my wings began to droop. I was so scared and lonely; I tucked myself into a little hole in a tree and cried myself to sleep."

"Oh, no! Poor Dayana."

"Then, one night, I flew to the edge of the garden and sat atop a sculpture of a fish with a funny face. Imagine my surprise when, just after nightfall, the sculpture moved, dumping me almost all the way to the ground!"

"Were you hurt?" asked Cassidy.

"I was too excited to worry about skinning my wings or bruising my bum!"

"That night, I watched as all the sculptures broke free of their pedestals. Little men played the softest music as colorful fish swam circles in the air, creating their own ballet."

"Dogs with very serious faces jumped and ran, trying to steal sticks from one another."

"Three ladies walked by, laughing and giggling, when suddenly, one got a running start and executed a series of perfect backflips. The other two tried but just splatted on the ground."

"I wish I could do a backflip!" Cassidy said.

"We all played until the sun peeked over the horizon. Then, I heard a far-away singing. I couldn't hear the words, but they came from the West, coaxing the sun higher and higher. All my new friends scattered and ran back to their pedestals."

All, except for Dayana, became statues again.

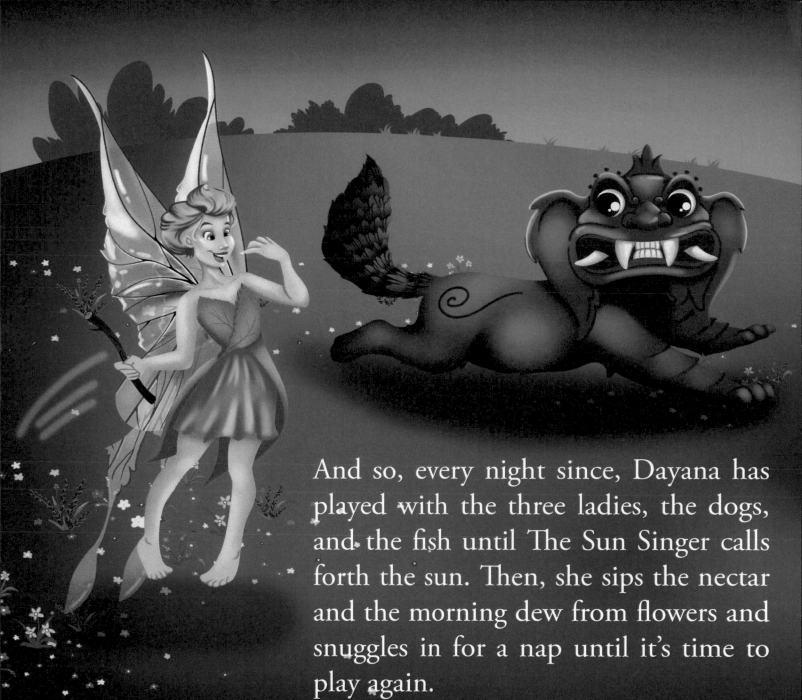

And so, every night since, Dayana has played with the three ladies, the dogs, and the fish until The Sun Singer calls forth the sun. Then, she sips the nectar and the morning dew from flowers and snuggles in for a nap until it's time to play again.

"But don't you get bored and lonely?" Cassidy asked.

"Oh, no," Dayana said, "because every day is new. Every day the flowers are different, the trees are different, and my friends all want to play different games."

"The most important thing to remember is:
My favorite fun just doesn't hide
With friends or Mom or Dad
Or with the best toy you've ever had.

Fun comes from deep inside
You have to find it in
yourself... and slide."

Cassidy was about to ask another question but she heard a voice calling, "Cassidy! Cassidy, where are you?"

It was her Daddy! With a flutter and a flip, Dayana disappeared as Daddy stuck his head inside the hedge.

"What are you doing in here, pumpkin?" he asked. "Are you ready to go find Mommy? It's time to go home."

"I have so much to tell you," Cassidy said. "Did you know the fish and the dog statues come alive at night and run around playing with each other?"

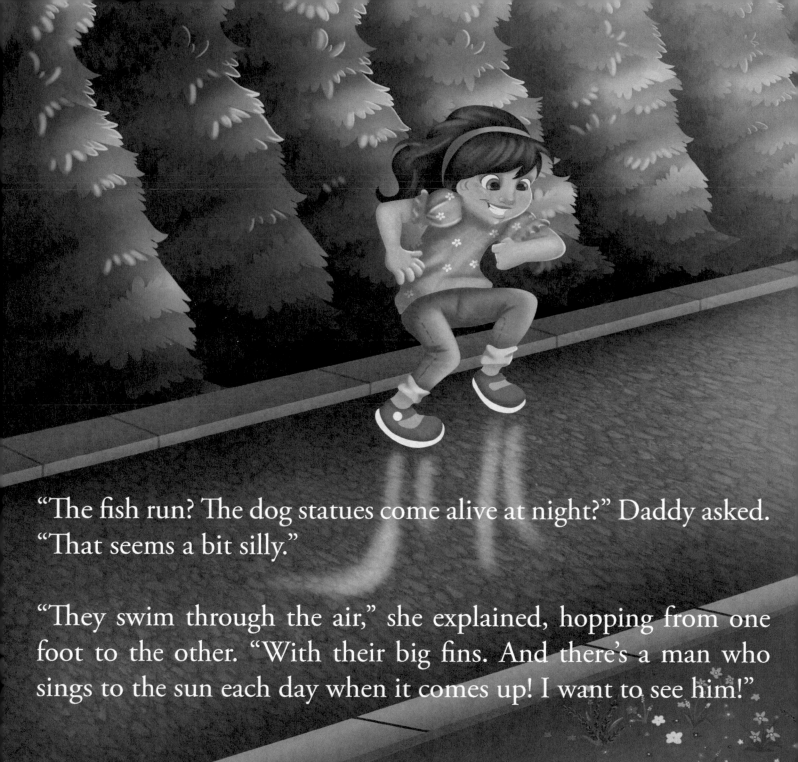

"The fish run? The dog statues come alive at night?" Daddy asked. "That seems a bit silly."

"They swim through the air," she explained, hopping from one foot to the other. "With their big fins. And there's a man who sings to the sun each day when it comes up! I want to see him!"

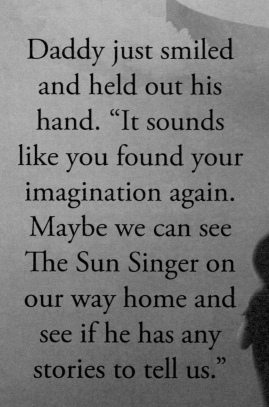

Daddy just smiled and held out his hand. "It sounds like you found your imagination again. Maybe we can see The Sun Singer on our way home and see if he has any stories to tell us."

Cassidy smiled and grabbed his hand. She felt sure she wasn't going to be bored for a very long time.

About Allerton Park

Allerton Park & Retreat Center is a real place near Monticello in central Illinois. It's considered one of the Seven Wonders of Illinois, but the author just discovered it a few years ago as a beautiful place to hike and take photographs.

It was built in 1899 by Robert Allerton, a philanthropist, farmer and art collector. He continuously added art and sculptures to his estate, bringing pieces home from Europe and Asia to enhance his beloved, carefully designed gardens, which today display more than 100 ornaments. Allerton enjoyed hiking through the woods and gardens and often invited friends, family, artists, journalists and others to visit.

In 1946, Allerton donated his home to the University of Illinois so others could enjoy his art and learn about nature and science on this special 1,500 acre parcel. More than 100,000 people visit Allerton Park & Retreat Center each year.

Made in the USA
Monee, IL
08 June 2020